HAWKEYE COLLINS & AMY ADAMS in

THE SECRET OF THE

VIDEO GAME SCORES

& OTHER MYSTERIES

by M. MASTERS

S0-ARK-636

Meadowbrook Books
18318 Minnetonka Blvd.
Deephaven, MN 55391

This book is dedicated to all the children across the country who helped us develop the *Can You Solve the Mystery?*™ series.

Library of Congress Cataloging in Publication Data

Masters, M.
    Hawkeye Collins & Amy Adams in The secret of the video game scores & other mysteries.

    (Can you solve the mystery? ; v. 12)
    Summary: Two twelve-year-old sleuths solve ten mysteries using Hawkeye's sketches of important clues.   [1. Mystery and detective stories]   I. Title.   II. Title: Hawkeye Collins and Amy Adams in The secret of the video game scores & other mysteries.   III. Title: Secret of the video game scores & other mysteries.   IV. Series: Masters, M.   Can you solve the mystery ; v. 12.
PZ7.M42392Hp   1984   [Fic]   83-26554

ISBN 0-88166-026-4 (pbk.)

10   9   8   7   6   5   4   3   2   1
Printed in the United States of America.

Copyright ©1984 by Meadowbrook Creations.

"The Mystery of the Speedy Snitcher" by Paul Bagdon.
All other stories by B. B. Hiller.
Editorial services by Parachute Press, Inc.
Illustrations by Brett Gadbois.
Cover art by Robert Sauber.

CONTENTS

READ THE SOLUTIONS IN YOUR MIRROR

*Would you like to become a member of
the CYSTM?™ Reading Panel?
See details on page 95.*

Amy Adams

Hawkeye Collins

Young Sleuths Detect Fun in Mysteries

By Alice Cory
Staff Writer

Lakewood Hills has two new super sleuths watching over its citizens. They are Christopher "Hawkeye" Collins and Amy Amanda Adams, both 12 years old and sixth-grade students at Lakewood Hills Elementary.

Christopher Collins, the popular, blond, blue-eyed sleuth of 128 Crestview Drive, is better known by his nickname, "Hawkeye." His father, Peter Collins, who is an attorney downtown, explains, "We started calling him Hawkeye many years ago because he notices everything, even tiny details. That's what makes him so good at solving mysteries." His mother, Linda Collins, a real estate agent, agrees: "Yes, but he

Sleuths continued on page 4A

Sleuths continued from page 2A

also started to draw at a very early age. His sketches capture everything he sees. He draws clues or the scene of the crime — or anything else that will help solve a mystery."

Amy Adams, a spitfire with red hair and sparkling green eyes, lives right across the street, at 131 Crestview Drive. Known to many as the star of the track team, she is also a star math student. "She's quick of mind, quick of foot and quick of temper," says her teacher, Ted Bronson, chuckling. "And she's never intimidated." Not only do she and Hawkeye share the same birthday, but also the same love of mysteries.

"If something's wrong," says Amy, leaning on her ten-speed, "you just can't look the other way."

"Right," says Hawkeye, pulling his ever-present sketch pad and pencil from his back pocket. "And if we can't solve a case right away, I'll do a drawing of the scene of the crime. When we study my sketch, we can usually figure out what happened."

When the two detectives are not playing video games or soccer (Hawkeye is the captain of the sixth-grade team), they can often be seen biking around town, making sure justice is done. Occa-sionally aided by Hawkeye's frisky golden retriever, Nosey, and Amy's six-year-old sister, Lucy, they've solved every case they've handled to date.

How did the two get started in the detective business?

It all started last year at Lakewood Hills Elementary's Career Days. There the two met Sergeant Treadwell, one of Lakewood Hills' best-known policemen. Of Hawkeye and Amy, Sergeant Treadwell proudly brags, "They're terrific. Right after we met, one of the teachers had a whole pile of tests stolen. I sure couldn't figure out who had done it, but Hawkeye did one of his sketches and he and Amy had the case solved in five minutes! You can't fool those two."

Sergeant Treadwell adds: "I don't know what Lakewood Hills ever did without Hawkeye and Amy. They've found a dognapped dog, located stolen video games, and cracked many other tough cases. Why, whenever I have a problem I can't solve, I know just where to go — straight to those two super sleuths!"

> **" They've found a dognapped dog, located stolen video games, and cracked many other tough cases. "**

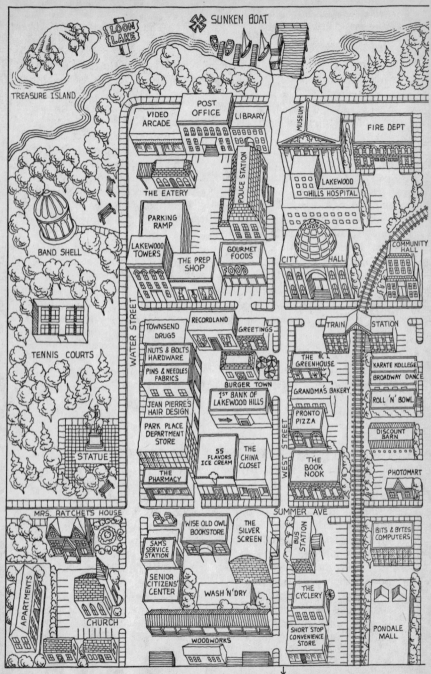

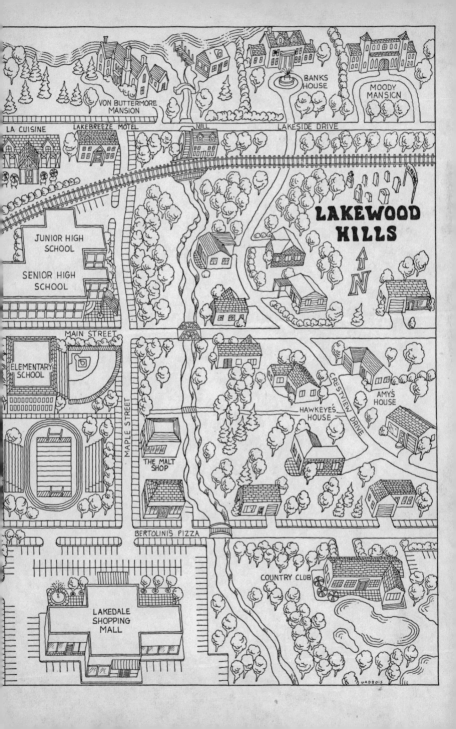

Dear Readers,

You can solve these mysteries along with us! Start by reading very carefully -- Watch out for things like what people <u>say</u> happened, the ways they behave, and details like the time and the weather.

Then look closely at the sketch or other picture clue with the story. If you remember the facts, the picture clue should help you break the case.

If you want to check your answer-- or if a hard case stumps you -- turn to the solutions at the back of the book. They're written in mirror type. Hold them up to a mirror and they'll look right. If you don't have a mirror, turn the page and hold it up to the light. (You can teach yourself to read backwards, too. We can do it pretty well now and it comes in handy some- times in our cases.)

Have fun -- we sure did !

Amy

Hawkeye

The Secret of the Fortune-Teller

Hawkeye Collins looked at his best friend, Amy Adams. "What did you just say?"

Amy sighed impatiently. "I said that everything's hunky-dory for going to the Video Arcade this afternoon."

"That's a funny expression," said Hawkeye.

He and Amy were known in their hometown of Lakewood Hills, Minnesota, as super sleuths. The two sixth graders were good at solving mysteries and sometimes even helped their local police department find the solutions to crimes. They both noticed unusual things.

"Yeah, it is funny," Amy agreed. "I guess I picked it up from one of my mom's patients. He was leaving her office as I arrived, and I heard him say, 'Don't worry about it, Dr. Adams. I've got it on good authority that everything will be fine—hunky-dory, in fact!'

"I asked my mom if there was a problem. She reminded me that she can't discuss details of her patients' illnesses, but she did say that Mr. Selden really needs an operation before his condition gets worse. At first, he agreed, but he changed his mind—like that!" Amy snapped her fingers.

"That must have upset your mom."

"It did, but she can't force him to have the operation. It's his decision. The weird thing is that he's absolutely *sure* he's going to be OK without the surgery."

Suddenly Hawkeye slapped himself on the forehead. "I forgot! Mrs. von Buttermore called. She wants us to come out and see her. She said she's got some 'wonderful but mysterious' news."

Mrs. von Buttermore was the richest woman in town and a very special friend of Hawkeye and Amy's.

"Maybe the news is about her dog, Priceless," Amy said. "Can you believe some driver couldn't see that huge Great Dane in front of his car? Mrs. von Buttermore's been really worried about him. He's been in the animal hospital for a week."

"I hope that *is* her news," said Hawkeye. "But I wonder what could be mysterious about it."

"Let's go see her. I'll race you!" Amy yelled, already halfway to her bike.

They hopped onto their ten-speeds and were at the von Buttermore mansion in minutes. Before ringing the doorbell, Amy picked a small bouquet of wildflowers for their friend.

"Oh, how lovely!" said Mrs. von Buttermore when she opened the door. "They'll look so pretty on my table tonight—for the celebration."

Amy's eyebrows shot up. "What are you celebrating?"

"Well, it's Priceless. You see—"

"He's going to get well?" Amy interrupted. "Dr. Rodrigues must have called! Hey, that's great!"

"Not exactly," said Mrs. von Buttermore. "Actually, the vet still isn't sure, but *I* am. Priceless is going to be just fine!"

Amy looked puzzled.

"Mrs. von Buttermore," Hawkeye asked, "how do you know? Is that your mysterious news?"

"Oh, my dears, it's the most wonderful thing! I hardly believed it myself, but the evidence was there. It *has* to be true!" Then Mrs. von Buttermore told them the whole story.

She had been at Jean Pierre's Hair Design, having her nails done. The manicurist, Marie, had asked why she was so depressed, and Mrs. von Buttermore had told her about Priceless.

"Dear Marie—she's such a nice person. She

understood how upset I was about not knowing what was going to happen to Priceless. She suggested that I see a fortune-teller. She said she'd seen one who had helped her with a problem about her cat, Roger. Well, the idea sounded a little silly to me, and Mrs. Selden, who was sitting next to me, thought so, too. But Marie just kept talking about this wonderful Madam Bertha, who could see into the future. Finally, I decided it wouldn't hurt anything for me to visit the fortune-teller."

Amy shot Hawkeye a look when the name Selden was mentioned, but before she could say anything, the butler brought in iced tea and cookies. While he served them, Mrs. von Buttermore continued with her story.

"Marie gave me a letter of introduction to Madam Bertha. It was a nice note, although Marie misspelled several words.

"I think Mrs. Selden was also worried about some problem. She listened very carefully to everything Marie said, and as I left, I saw Marie give her a note, too."

"So what was Madam Bertha like?" Amy asked eagerly. "Did she tell your fortune?"

"Oh, she was wonderful!" exclaimed Mrs. von Buttermore. "As soon as she uncovered her crystal ball, she said, 'Your dog! There is danger!' She told me she could hear the screech of the car tires. It was terrible to relive that moment when Priceless was hurt, but Madam Bertha *saw* it right there in her magic crystal ball."

"Did she explain *how* she could see it in her crystal ball?" asked Hawkeye.

"No—that's the mystery, isn't it?" Mrs. von Buttermore beamed at them. "I usually don't believe in this kind of thing, but when she could see the past so clearly, I *knew* I could rely on her predictions. Then she told me she had good news for me: Priceless will be fine. The woman is amazing! I was so impressed that I gave her a thousand dollars so she could continue her psychic studies and help others as she helped me."

Mrs. von Buttermore's eyes twinkled as she imitated Madam Bertha. " 'Your dok vill be vell. Effryting vill be—how you say?—hunky-dory.' "

Hawkeye and Amy couldn't help laughing at Mrs. von Buttermore's accent.

While Mrs. von Buttermore refilled their glasses, Amy noticed that Hawkeye was deep in thought. "What are you thinking, Hawkeye?" she asked.

"I'm thinking that I'd like to take a look at that note Marie wrote. Do you still have it, Mrs. von Buttermore?"

"Why, yes, I do. It's upstairs." She had the maid bring it to him.

Hawkeye and Amy both studied the note for a while.

"Well, it's all here," said Hawkeye finally. "Some words are misspelled, but some other things

Bertha: Please help my friend, Mrs. von Buttermore.

Do ONE GOOD HELPFULL ITEM TODAY. BERTHA, YOU'RE CAREFULL, ABLE, RARE.

Marie

P.S. ROGER IS CATNIP HAPPY!

"But Marie just kept talking about this Madam Bertha, who could see into the future," said Mrs. von Buttermore.

are crystal clear. Mrs. von Buttermore, Madam Bertha and Marie have tricked you out of a thousand bucks and probably put Mr. Selden into a lot of danger!"

WHY DID HAWKEYE THINK MRS. VON BUTTERMORE HAD BEEN TRICKED?

See page 65

The Mystery of the Circus Kidnapping

"*This* is where I want to sit!" insisted Lucy, Amy's six-year-old sister. "And I want some cotton candy and some peanuts, and . . ." As Lucy went on with her list of food, Amy wondered, for the tenth time, why she had ever agreed to bring her little sister to the circus. She was glad that Hawkeye, her best friend and fellow detective, had come, too. It seemed that wherever they went together, they ended up being involved in a mystery. But what mystery could there be at the circus?

By the time the bears and the clowns were done performing, Lucy had had all the junk food she wanted and was happy. Then the ringmaster stepped up to his microphone.

"Ladies and gentlemen. Due to circumstances beyond our control, the great Rosalita and her perfect pair of ponies, Peg and Sis, will not appear at today's performance."

Amy and Hawkeye looked at each other. Anything out of the ordinary always caught their attention. Before they could discuss the announcement, a woman tapped Hawkeye's shoulder.

"Are you two Hawkeye Collins and Amy Adams? Could you come with me?" she asked. "We heard you were good at solving mysteries, and we need your help!"

Amy told Lucy to stay where she was, and their next-door neighbor, who happened to be sitting next to Lucy, agreed to keep an eye on her.

"What's this all about?" Hawkeye asked once they were outside.

"I'm Frieda Wosniak, and I own this circus," said the woman. "We've got a problem. I called the police and talked to a Sergeant Treadwell. He'll be here as soon as possible, but he told me you were in the audience and could probably help until he arrives."

"We'll try. What's wrong?"

"It's Rosalita's pony. She has two, Peg and Sis, a perfectly matched pair, but Peg's been kidnapped. Someone's holding the pony for ten thousand dollars ransom!"

"That's rotten!" exclaimed Amy. "Who'd do something like that?"

10

"A ransom note was found in the clowns' trailer. All the trailers are locked during the shows, so the note couldn't have been left in Rosalita's trailer. Since only the clowns have keys to their own trailer and they all dislike Rosalita, we think one of them is the kidnapper. But we don't know which one."

The two young sleuths were very surprised. They had seen the clowns perform, and it was hard to believe the hilarious figures in bright makeup and big, floppy shoes would dislike *anyone*.

"Come along, and I'll introduce you to Rosalita. Then I'll show you the note."

Amy and Hawkeye followed Ms. Wosniak through the maze of tents and trailers. It was hard to remember that before the circus had arrived, this had been just a large, empty field outside town. Now it was almost a small town in itself.

The circus owner stopped outside a small trailer. "Here we are. Rosalita, I'd like you to meet Lakewood Hills' famous detectives, Hawkeye Collins and Amy Adams. I'm told that if anyone can help us, they can."

"Pah! What can two *children* do?" Rosalita glared at Amy and Hawkeye. "My wonderful pony is gone forever. Leave me alone! I'll see no one but the chief of police."

Hawkeye and Amy shrugged their shoulders and turned away.

"Is she always so unfriendly?" Amy asked

Ms. Wosniak as they crossed the circus lot again.

Ms. Wosniak explained that Rosalita was a very temperamental star.

"Does that mean she has a lot of enemies?" asked Hawkeye.

"It'd be kinder to say she doesn't have many friends. It's the worst with the clowns. At first Rosalita was friendly with them. Then one by one, she made them all angry because of her practical jokes, her cruel remarks, and her rudeness. Now it looks as if one of the clowns is paying her back."

The circus owner nodded toward a colorful wagon. "This is it—the clowns' trailer."

Hawkeye and Amy stepped inside and looked around in amazement at the jumble of costumes and props. The shelves were crowded with books about clowning, and the closets bulged with scarves, hats, and costumes.

"It's such a small trailer that there's only one makeup table," said Ms. Wosniak. "Look, there's the note."

The ransom note was written in clown makeup and was taped to the makeup table mirror. It read, "Rosalita, I have your pony. I want $10,000. Instructions to follow."

Hawkeye turned from the note to Ms. Wosniak. "I'd like to look around a little."

"Why don't you sketch the scene, too, Hawkeye?" suggested Amy. "Your sharp eyes pick up every detail when you draw."

The ransom note was written in clown makeup and taped to the makeup table mirror.

Hawkeye pulled out his sketch pad and drew the makeup table and mirror.

"Since it looks like the pony was taken by one of the clowns, Ms. Wosniak," Amy said, "you'd better tell us about them."

"They're a real bunch of jokers," said the circus owner, "but I feel lucky to have them. Frank, Burt, and Mario have been with me for years. Elton and Lefty joined us three years ago and developed that funny baseball skit you saw. I hired Butch and Juan last year and Pierre this season. I can't imagine one of them taking that pony."

Hawkeye and Amy asked a few more questions and learned that the pony had disappeared right after the show started. But because there had been so much happening when the show began, it was impossible to track down who was where at that time.

For a moment, Hawkeye thought he and Amy might be stumped, but then he held up his sketch pad to look at the drawing again.

"Hey, I think— Amy! Look at this!"

"What's that, Hawkeye? Hmmmm. I see what you mean. I think you've got it!"

WHAT DID HAWKEYE AND AMY SEE IN THE SKETCH?

See page 69

The Case of the Invisible Burglar

"Hi, Mr. Fortunati," Amy called out as she walked into the Pronto Pizza restaurant on West Street in Lakewood Hills.

"Hello, Amy," answered the cheerful restaurant owner from behind the counter. "What's new with you?"

"Sergeant Treadwell asked Hawkeye and me to meet him here today to discuss the burglary at the China Closet store last night. The police are stumped by this one!"

Sergeant Treadwell was a member of the Lakewood Hills Police Department. He both respected and admired Hawkeye's and Amy's sleuthing abilities. He often talked over cases with them, and they had helped him solve a number of local crimes. Sarge and his two young friends shared not only detective work but also a love of pizza and hot fudge sundaes.

Mr. Fortunati smiled at Amy. "Sometimes I wonder if the Lakewood Hills police ever do anything without the help of you and Hawkeye," he teased her. "And speaking of your partner, here he comes. Hi, Hawkeye."

"Hello, Mr. Fortunati," said Hawkeye as he slid onto a chair next to Amy's.

"Hey, Mr. Fortunati," said Amy, "Hawkeye and I stopped by for a snack last night after the roller rink closed—at nine-thirty—but you were closed, too. We thought you always stayed open till midnight."

"Oh, we do."

"Not last night," Hawkeye protested. "Where were you?"

"I was over at the KLH radio station. Ellen Markville, the advertising director there, finally convinced me to make some radio commercials about my restaurant. KLH is offering a special deal to the businesses in town: a store gets a free commercial if the station can use pictures of the store or the employees in its own billboard campaign. Ms. Markville has been signing up all the stores on this street."

Mr. Fortunati suddenly looked embarrassed. "Now, don't laugh, but she told me that I have a perfect radio voice and that I should do the commercials myself. I thought she was being silly, but she's such a nice woman that it's hard to say no to her."

"I heard about the radio station offer," Amy said. "I thought KLH was signing up only the stores around the corner on Summer Avenue, like the bookstore and the movie theater—a kind of trial run to see how the whole thing works out."

Mr. Fortunati shrugged his shoulders. "I don't know about that. I only know Ms. Markville made me feel like I'd signed up to be a star!"

"Was it fun?" asked Hawkeye.

"Well, yes, but it was a little boring rehearsing and rehearsing—" The restaurant owner stopped and gestured toward the door. "Ah, here comes Sergeant Treadwell."

Hawkeye and Amy filled in Sarge about Mr. Fortunati's new career as a radio personality.

"So that's why you weren't open!" Sarge exclaimed. "I was hungry after the investigation of the burglary around the corner, so I stopped by."

"Sounds as if you lost a lot of business last night," Hawkeye told Mr. Fortunati.

"Well, I wanted to record the commercial at another time, but Ms. Markville said it *had* to be last night—something about the sound engineer not being available. Then, wouldn't you know, she didn't show up until it was too late for us to finish. She had to rush off to another appointment, and all I got to do was to rehearse. Pete, my manager, and I have to go back tonight to make the actual commercial."

"Enough chatter," said Sergeant Treadwell. "I'm really hungry, and I bet these sleuths are, too, right?"

"Yes, sir!" Amy and Hawkeye agreed.

"OK, Mr. Fortunati, let's have some pizzas here," Sarge said as he moved toward the counter. "This is my treat, so I'll do the ordering. Hawkeye and Amy can wait and be surprised."

"Just remember one thing about *my* pizza," Amy called out anxiously.

"We know!" said the policeman and the restaurant owner together. "NO PEPPERONI!"

To pass the time, Hawkeye pulled his sketch pad out of his back pocket and started drawing. He carefully sketched the scene across West Street that Mr. Fortunati looked at every day through the windows of his restaurant.

"OK, kids, our pizzas are cooking!" said Sergeant Treadwell. "Let's talk about the burglary while we wait. Here's the story. Last night, someone got inside the China Closet store about ten o'clock, but we can't find any sign of forced entry. You can see the back of the store right across the street." He pointed out the windows at the scene Hawkeye had sketched a few minutes before.

"Anyway, the burglar got away with a matched set of very valuable antique figurines.

"The strangest part is that nobody saw anything. There was a big crowd at the movie last night," said Hawkeye.

There were crowds of people right across from the store at the movie theater on Summer Avenue, and next door to the store at the ice cream shop, but apparently nobody saw anything."

Sarge paused for a moment to sniff the delicious smell of baking pizza.

He sighed and went back to his story. "We thought maybe it was a fake burglary to collect the insurance money. But it turns out that the owner hasn't been able to get theft insurance because he's been robbed before."

"Ummm," said Hawkeye. "The strangest part is that nobody in the area saw anything."

Amy turned to the restaurant owner. "What about you, Mr. Fortunati? Did you see— No, of course not. You were at the radio station."

Sarge shook his head. "We're beginning to think we may have an invisible crook in town."

"Hawkeye," said Amy, "I've got an idea. Let me have a look at that sketch you just did."

Amy and Hawkeye studied the sketch silently. Then Amy's eyes lit up. "Got it!" she said. "Your burglar wasn't invisible, Sarge, just clever."

HOW WAS THE BURGLARY COMMITTED?

See page 73

The Secret of the Video Game Scores

"Hey, nice going, Toni!" said Amy Adams to her cousin. "Ten more hours of practice and you'll be *almost* as good at this Crazy Caterpillar game as I am!"

Amy's cousin looked disappointed as she answered, "Thanks, Amy, but it would probably take more than that. I still can't break 30,000 points."

"Look, I've got four tokens left," Amy said. "Let's have one final game before the Crazy Caterpillar Derby on Sunday, OK?"

"Sure, but why can't we come back for more practice tomorrow?" asked Toni.

"Well, aside from the fact that I'm out of money, tomorrow's Saturday. You and I are going to rake leaves for Grandma Adams, remember? So this is it, kid! This is the final match between the Lakewood Hills Crazy Caterpillar video game runner-up—that's yours truly—and her up-and-coming young cousin, the seventh-best player in town, Toni Jane Adams!"

"OK, Amy, one more game!"

The girls dropped in their tokens and the game began. Even though Toni's caterpillar managed to spin six cocoons, eat eighteen mulberries, zap three slugs, and fly through four spiderwebs, Amy still won the game. Almost nobody could beat Amy at dodging butterfly nets.

Later the cousins raced back home on their ten-speeds. Toni won, and that seemed fair to Amy. She hated to see her cousin upset about the Crazy Caterpillar Derby. They parted at Amy's driveway, agreeing to meet at nine o'clock the next morning to get to their grandmother's by ten.

Their plans didn't work out, however. At eight o'clock Saturday morning, Amy's phone rang. When she answered it, a voice whispered something she couldn't understand.

"What?" said Amy. "Who is this?"

"Toni." The word was just a hoarse croak. "I have a sore throat."

"Boy, you sure do!" said Amy. "Well, don't worry. I'll go to Grandma's by myself—which means I'll get to eat all of her great apple pie by myself, too!"

There was a slight squeak on the other end of the phone.

"No, don't talk, Toni. Just take care of yourself. I hope you'll be OK by tomorrow for the video game derby," Amy said.

"Me, too," rasped Toni. "Bye."

So Amy went to her grandmother's house by herself. She really didn't mind. She enjoyed spending time alone with Grandma Adams. Although she raked leaves until she had blisters on her hands, she still had an hour to hear some of her grandmother's stories about when Amy's father was a boy.

They laughed together over the stories. Amy never told her dad about them—they were a secret with Grandma Adams—but she found it very comforting to know that he hadn't always been perfect. Sometimes the things her dad had done even reminded Amy of herself.

"Some things never change, my dear," said her grandmother. "Now, how about another slice of apple pie? I think I have some more vanilla ice cream."

It was a pleasant day, but Amy was tired when she finally got home. She wanted to have dinner and then get a good night's sleep before the derby.

After dinner, Amy called Toni to tell her about the day and to see how she was feeling. Amy was pleased to hear her cousin talking so well.

"Great," said Amy. "I guess what you needed was a day in bed. So you should be OK for the derby tomorrow, right?"

"Oh, sure," Toni agreed. "Thanks for calling. I'll see you at the Video Arcade at one o'clock tomorrow. Bye."

When Amy hung up, she looked longingly at the bathtub. She thought a nice long soak in it would be just the right way to end the day. Her plan was interrupted, however, by the phone ringing.

"Amy, it's me." Amy recognized Hawkeye's voice.

"What's up, Hawkeye?"

"I've got a present for you," he said.

"Can you give it to me tomorrow? I'm really tired." She explained about raking all day.

"No, you need it before tomorrow. It'll psyche you up for the derby."

"OK, come on over," Amy said good-naturedly.

In a few minutes, the doorbell rang.

"Hi," Hawkeye said, looking at his tired friend. "Here's your present. I was passing by the Video Arcade on my way home this evening, and I went inside to check the Crazy Caterpillar game ratings. I made a sketch of the ratings from the screen. I thought you should have the latest scores so you know what you have to aim for tomorrow. Boy, both you and Toni are doing great! Amy,

"Oh, it is a perfect picture," said Amy. "A perfect picture of a rat!"

you're in the number two position."

"Gee, thanks, Hawkeye," Amy said as she glanced at the scores. "I really appreci—" Amy stopped and looked closely at the sketch.

"Why, of all the scheming, low-down, dirty, rotten, mean—"

"Hey, I know it's not a perfect work of art, Amy, but what's the matter?"

"Oh, it *is* a perfect picture," said Amy. "A perfect picture of a rat!"

WHY WAS AMY SO ANGRY?

SOLUTION

See page 77

The Case of the Escaped Convict

Amy Adams answered the phone on the second ring.

"Hi, Amy. It's Hawkeye."

"Oh, hi. What's up?"

"Lots!" Hawkeye exclaimed. "Sarge just called me."

"So, what did he want?"

"Diane Simpson's father!"

"What are you talking about, Hawkeye? Her dad was convicted of armed robbery a year ago."

"Sure—but he just broke out of prison."

"Oh, no! But why did Sarge call you?"

"He wants us to go with him when he talks to Mrs. Simpson. The news about the jailbreak will probably upset Diane and her mother, and Sarge thought it would be a good idea for Diane to have some friends there. He'll pick us up in five minutes. OK, Amy?"

"OK. See you in five minutes."

As Amy marked her place in the book she'd been reading and ran a comb through her red hair, she thought about what it had been like for Diane Simpson during her father's trial. Amy, Hawkeye, and Diane's other classmates had tried to be especially kind to her, but it had been a hard time for Diane.

Amy told her parents where she was going and left the house quickly. As she and Hawkeye met in the warm June evening, she could tell they'd both been thinking about the same thing.

"Poor Diane," said Hawkeye.

"Yeah," answered Amy. "Remember how upset she was during the trial? It was bad enough for her to have her dad in jail, but it was really rotten for her to have to read about it in the paper every day!"

"I'm glad Sarge asked us along. Here he comes."

As they drove to the Simpson house, Sarge filled Hawkeye and Amy in. The police didn't know if Simpson was going to try to sneak out of the country or if he would try to get to his family. They wanted to find out if his wife and daughter knew where he was. But if the family didn't know anything, then the police didn't want them upset. That's why Sarge had asked Amy and Hawkeye to come along.

When they got to the house, Mrs. Simpson was cooking dinner, and Diane was setting the table. The five people stood in the kitchen while Sarge explained what was going on. As he spoke, the blood drained from Mrs. Simpson's face, and she sank into a chair.

"Mexico," she said. "My husband always talked about Mexico."

"You think that's where he'll go?" Sarge asked.

"Where else?"

Amy could see that Diane was shaken by the news about her father. "Come on, Diane. Let's go up to your room, where we can talk." Together, the two girls left the kitchen.

Hawkeye stayed with Sarge. Feeling something like a third wheel, he took out his sketch pad and drew the kitchen while Sarge and Mrs. Simpson continued to talk.

"I was just making dinner for Diane and me," said Mrs. Simpson. "Now I don't know if I can even eat. What's going to happen, Sergeant?"

"Well, if you're pretty sure your husband is headed for Mexico, we'll concentrate on looking for him on the southern routes."

"Yes, Mexico. Do that," she answered.

Just then, Amy and Diane reappeared.

As Sarge spoke, the blood drained from Mrs. Simpson's face, and she sank into a chair.

"Did you girls have a talk?" asked Sarge.

"Yes," answered Amy. "We ended up sitting in the den." She smiled at Diane. "Diane has as much trouble keeping her room neat as I do."

"My—my room's a mess right now," Diane stuttered. "I'm airing out all my winter clothes."

Mrs. Simpson looked uncomfortable. Amy thought the woman was probably upset at having strangers see her house when it wasn't neat.

Hawkeye's mind was racing. He pulled out his sketch pad to glance at his drawing.

"Sarge," he said suddenly, "I've got to get back home now. Can we go?"

Amy looked at her friend. It wasn't like Hawkeye to hurry at such a moment. She suspected that he must be onto a clue.

As they left, Sarge said, "I'd better get on the radio. The state police will need to cover the southern routes, the bus stations, airports—"

"Hold it, Sarge," interrupted Hawkeye. "You're going to need the state police—but probably right here in Lakewood Hills."

"I knew it!" Amy exclaimed. "Hawkeye, you saw something! What was it?"

"Well, it was a pretty good snow job, but nobody should try to pull the wool over my eyes!"

WHAT DID HAWKEYE SEE?

See page 79

31

The Mystery of the Speedy Snitcher

Sergeant Treadwell looked stern and official as he sat behind his desk at the Lakewood Hills Police Department headquarters. He waved a pretzel absentmindedly as he spoke.

"Ken Thomas," Sarge said, "has been bad news—and nothing but bad news—ever since he and his family moved to Lakewood Hills. You two know that."

Hawkeye Collins sat in a straight-backed chair, his long legs extended in front of him. "I guess you're right, Sarge," he said. "That's why all the kids call him Bad News Thomas. He'd only lived here four months when Amy and I helped you figure out that he was the one who T.P.'d Mr.

Bronson's house to get back at him for that *F* in social studies."

Amy Adams nodded in agreement. "And," she said, "it was only a couple of weeks later that the store detective at the Prep Shop caught him trying to rip off a pair of cords and two sweaters."

"Right, Amy," Sarge said, "and there have been several—no, many—other happenings. Bad News was taking milk and dessert money from the day-care and kindergarten kids before school let out. And he tried to steal three albums from Recordland over on Main Street."

"Have you tried talking to his folks, Sarge?" Hawkeye asked.

"Yes, I have. You know I always try to give a young person a better-than-even break. The Thomases are the finest, most upright people you'll ever meet. They're worried sick about their son, but they don't understand Bad News any better than I do—or apparently than anyone else does, for that matter. I just can't figure what it is that makes a youngster turn bad."

Sarge sighed and waited for the clatter and rumble of a train pulling past City Hall, about a block away, to die down. "When I spoke with Mr. and Mrs. Thomas about a month ago—in front of Bad News—I told all of them that there would be no more chances, and no more warnings. I said it was my duty as a police officer to recommend that Bad News be put into a state reform facility if he got into trouble again. I *warned* him what would happen. I even suggested psychiatric help. Mr. Thomas told me he'd made several appointments for Bad News to see a counselor at Lakewood Hills Hospital who specializes in the problems of young people. Bad News didn't keep a single one of the appointments."

"And?" Amy asked, her red hair shifting as she leaned forward in her chair, waiting for Sarge's answer.

"And," Sarge responded, "he blew it—and blew it very badly this time. He stole over two hundred dollars from the Sun 'n' Fun swimming and recreation center Saturday morning. Mr. and Mrs. Lindbloom, the owners of Sun 'n' Fun, saw Bad News scoop the money out of their cash register. They both made positive identifications. They said they always watch him closely when he comes into their place; they know he has sticky fingers."

Hawkeye looked confused. "But then why did you call Amy and me down here? I can't see what else you'd need to sew up the case—you have positive IDs from eyewitnesses. Isn't it an open-and-shut case?"

"Not at all, Hawkeye. Not at all. I need your skills—and Amy's. You see, when Bad News grabbed the cash at Sun 'n' Fun, it was exactly 11:00 A.M. The clock is directly above the cash register, and Mr. and Mrs. Lindbloom both noted the time. They're sure of it."

"And?" Amy asked, once again.

"Just this: at exactly 11:04, Bad News strolled into City Hall and asked Ellen Parks, the city clerk, about a dog license. Then he asked her what time it was. She told him it was 11:04. He asked if she was positive that it was 11:04, and she said yes. Bad News thanked her and left. Miss Parks also made a positive identification when I spoke with her."

"Sarge," Hawkeye said slowly, "Sun 'n' Fun is over a mile south of Lakewood Hills—and it's almost another two miles from the edge of town to City Hall. There's no way Bad News could have covered that distance on foot. That would be three miles in four minutes!"

Hawkeye couldn't help but grin. "Even Amy, the captain of our track team, isn't that fast."

Amy made a face at Hawkeye but ignored his comment. "I wonder," she said, "if Bad News could have hitchhiked and made it to City Hall that way."

"There are too many 'ifs' in that theory, Amy," Sarge said. "It won't hold up. And there's another point here: even if Bad News had swiped a car or moped and driven like crazy, he still couldn't have covered that route in four minutes on a Saturday. You know how the traffic is in town—cars and shoppers all over the place, freight trains holding up traffic for minutes at a time, kids on bikes. No, a car couldn't make it, either. I'm sure of that."

"This does not compute," said Amy. "Even a real hotdogger on the best ten-speed racer couldn't make that distance in four minutes. The two of us have biked out there to swim or to play video games lots of times. It's a *long* haul." Amy unconsciously twisted a strand of her hair as she followed her thought. "It just doesn't figure."

"Sarge," Hawkeye asked, "what are the odds that either the Lindblooms or Ellen Parks could be off on their times?"

"Very, very slim," answered Sarge. "But you can check that out when you talk to them. I believe the Lindblooms and Miss Parks are all excellent witnesses. That's the sole reason Bad News is free right now. How he did it, I don't know—but I *know* he did it."

Hawkeye stood up and brushed his blond hair from his forehead. "Well, Sarge," he said, "you have our word that we'll work on this one until we solve it. Amy, how about riding over to Bad News' house to see if he'll talk to us? I suppose it's a long shot, but we have to start somewhere."

"OK, Hawkeye, let's give it a try."

Bad News Thomas didn't look like a 13-year-old sixth grader. His dirty, shoulder-length hair and perpetual sneer combined to make him appear quite a bit older than his classmates.

"Well," Bad News said sarcastically as Amy and Hawkeye stopped their bikes in front of his porch, "if it ain't the Clark Kent and Lois Lane of Lakewood Hills. What do you want?"

"We'd like to talk to you about the Sun 'n' Fun," Hawkeye said.

Bad News' eyes narrowed. "Get lost, you turkeys! I did all the talking I'm going to do with that idiot Treadwell. I got nothin' to say to you. Now get!"

"Hey—" Amy began.

"Get!"

The next day, Hawkeye and Amy pedaled out to Sun 'n' Fun. The day was cool and clear, and there was very little traffic. They pushed themselves to maintain their best speed. The trip over the hilly route took nineteen minutes.

Mrs. Lindbloom set a large, cold cola in front of each of the sleuths.

"Oh, it was definitely Bad News Thomas," Mrs. Lindbloom said. "There's no doubt at all about that. My husband and I both were right here and saw him snatch the money and run out the door. Of course, we ran to the door, also, but he was gone. He had a little head start: we had to come all the way around the counter. But there's no mistake about Bad News or about the time. I hate to see a kid in trouble, but I've got to tell you the honest truth."

"We know that," said Amy gravely. "Thanks for your time—and for the drinks."

Amy and Hawkeye leaned against the counter in the city clerk's office in City Hall. Ellen Parks, a pretty, petite woman in her midtwenties, looked concerned.

"I can't tell you anything I didn't already tell Sarge," Miss Parks said. "Bad News came in here and asked me if this was the right place to get a dog license. Then he asked me for the time, told me to check again to see if it was exactly 11:04, and left. I know the time was right; my watch is less than a month old, and it's guaranteed to be correct within a couple of seconds a month. Sorry I can't be more help to you."

"Thanks anyway, Miss Parks," Hawkeye said.

Amy and Hawkeye sat on the steps outside City Hall. "I wonder if he used a hot air balloon or something!" exclaimed Amy.

Hawkeye sighed. "It's got to be *something* pretty far-out. I'm out of ideas."

"Well," said Amy slowly, "let's start with what we know—the path Bad News had to take. Why don't you sketch out the routes between Sun 'n' Fun and City Hall?"

"Sure," Hawkeye agreed doubtfully. In a moment, his pencil was moving about the page of the sketch pad he'd pulled from the back pocket of his

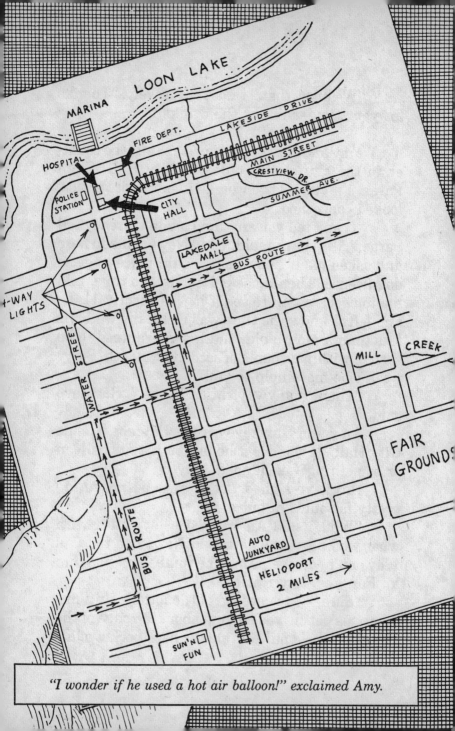

"I wonder if he used a hot air balloon!" exclaimed Amy.

jeans. Within a few minutes, he tore the page from the book and handed the drawing to Amy. "I tried to show the most logical routes, Amy, but I think you're going to be disappointed."

Amy studied the sketch.

Slowly, a broad smile replaced the strained look of intense concentration on her face. She lightly punched Hawkeye's shoulder. "You've done it again, Hawkeye," she said. "Your artwork has just solved another case. Let's get over to Sarge's office!"

WHAT DID AMY SEE THAT HELPED HER SOLVE THE CASE?

See page 81

The Case of the Convenient Car Crash

"Dad!" exclaimed Amy. "I'm so glad you're home! Do you think I should bring my parka or my poncho on our camping trip? Or do you think I should bring both? I can't wait till Friday. Flying with you, and then getting to spend two days at Tudor Lake! Wow, it's going to be—"

"Amy," Captain Adams said quietly, "I'm afraid I've got some disappointing news for you." He loosened his tie and dropped his jacket on a hall chair.

"Have they changed your schedule so you'll be flying over the weekend?" she asked. Captain Adams was an airline pilot, and Amy was used to sudden changes in his schedule, but she'd really been looking forward to two days alone with her father.

"No, it's not exactly a schedule change. I want to tell your mother about it, too. It's really a strange thing." They walked into the living room together and found Mary Adams there, filling out school health forms for her young patients.

"I need a good doctor's advice on this one," Amy's father said, going over to kiss the top of his wife's head.

Dr. Adams smiled at him. "I'm open for business."

"Well, you know I was in a small car accident yesterday. It didn't seem very serious at the time. It was raining and slippery, and my car slid into the Chevrolet in the next lane. We were both going about five miles an hour. My car had only a scratch, and the other car was slightly dented."

"A lot of people get hurt going five miles an hour," said Amy. She'd learned that in health class.

"That's true," said her father, "but we were all wearing seat belts—me, the other driver, and her husband, who was in the front passenger seat. Anyway, we all got out, inspected the damage, exchanged insurance information, and that seemed to be that."

"So?"

"So today, the man who was the passenger, Richard May, called me to say he'd been hurt in the accident after all. He broke his leg."

"You mean he broke his leg and didn't know it at the time?" asked Amy, astonished.

"Apparently," said Captain Adams. "He claims his shin was caught between the door and his seat. What do you say, Dr. Adams? Is that possible?"

"Well," said Amy's mother, "stranger things have occurred than for someone to walk around on a broken leg for a while. In fact, that did happen to a patient of mine."

"I'm very surprised that anybody got hurt," said Amy's father, "but I *am* responsible. Mr. May has a wife and two children. He's out of work, and now he has a broken leg."

He turned to Amy. "I'm really sorry about this, Amy, but I'm afraid we'll have to postpone our trip till another weekend. I feel I should go over to the Mays' home and do some of the yard work and house repairs that Mr. May can't handle now."

"But, Dad, we—" Amy stopped and swallowed hard. She knew her father was doing what he thought was right. "OK," she mumbled.

"Thanks, Amy. Don't worry. We'll have our camping weekend next month. I want to go just as much as you do!"

Captain Adams went to the Mays' house for a while on both Saturday and Sunday. On Monday, he flew to Chicago and stayed over. When he

"Richard May is suing me for a hundred thousand dollars!" said Mr. Adams.

came home Wednesday, there was a letter from Mr. May's insurance company waiting for him.

"Mary! Amy! Look at this!" he called. "Richard May is suing me for a hundred thousand dollars!"

"What?" said Dr. Adams. "How can he?"

"It says here that I was negligent in driving. I've caused Mr. May pain and suffering, and I've made it impossible for him to work."

The whole thing seemed pretty strange to Amy. First Mr. May was OK, and then his leg was broken. Her father had tried to be helpful, and now Mr. May was suing him.

She went into the den to talk with her father, who was staring at something in his hand.

"What's that, Dad?"

"A photograph I took of Mr. May, his wife, Susan, and their two children."

"But, Dad, you must have taken that a long time ago. And he must be accident-prone. I thought you just met him."

"I did just meet him," said Captain Adams.

"But that's impossible," said Amy, looking again at the photo to be sure. "Dad, I think you'd better call Hawkeye's father. You're going to need a lawyer."

WHAT DID AMY SEE IN THE PHOTOGRAPH?

S O L U T I O N

See page 83

The Secret of the Smashed Statue

Amy and Hawkeye were walking toward City Hall when Sergeant Treadwell pulled up next to them in his police cruiser.

"Hop in," he called. "We need you!" The two young sleuths looked at each other, surprised.

"What's up?" asked Hawkeye as he and Amy piled into the backseat.

"Vandalism at City Hall! Someone smashed the statue of Malcolm Forthwit, the founder of Lakewood Hills. The mayor's office called and said they were expecting you there this morning for the Good Citizen award ceremony, and they asked me to bring you over right away. Mayor Santini said, 'If they could figure out where an escaped convict

was hiding, surely they can figure out who broke the statue of Malcolm Forthwit!' "

Deputy Mayor Drummond met them at the curb. "Hello, Sergeant. Hawkeye and Amy, come right in. We've been waiting for you." They all hurried through the entrance to City Hall.

"There's the evidence!" announced the deputy mayor. Hawkeye and Amy looked at the corner where he pointed. Instead of the life-size statue of Forthwit's head, all they saw was an empty pedestal in front of a painting. On the floor, in about a dozen pieces, lay what remained of the Malcolm Forthwit statue.

Deputy Mayor Drummond continued. "Our cleaning woman, Ingrid West, found the pieces." He gestured to a woman leaning against the wall. "Ingrid and I came in at the same time this morning when I unlocked City Hall. She spotted the broken statue right away."

Just then, another man walked up to the group and asked what was going on.

"Who wants to know?" said Sergeant Treadwell quietly.

"I'm Martin Grafton. I painted that picture," he said, pointing to the painting behind the pedestal. "Not half bad, is it? Now that you can *see* it."

"We'll certainly be seeing a lot of it now," commented Deputy Mayor Drummond sarcastically.

Hawkeye's computerlike brain was working.

"It seems to me that we'll have to do some detective work, Amy," he said.

"Just what I was thinking," said Sarge. "But the question is, where do we begin?"

"I guess we begin with the basics," answered Amy. "We need to discover the means, the opportunity, and the motive for the vandalism. The means is easy—anyone could have knocked the statue off its pedestal. So let's work on opportunity. When did the crime happen? Who was the last person to see the statue unbroken?"

"I probably was," answered the deputy mayor. "I remember glancing at it on my way to a meeting with Mayor Santini at, oh, about six o'clock last night. City Hall was open, but I think we were the only ones in the building, except perhaps for Mrs. West. The mayor and I finished our meeting and left together about a half hour later. I locked up after us."

"Was the statue broken when you left?"

"Frankly, I didn't notice and neither did the mayor. We walked straight out. You have to look down that hallway to see the statue on your way out, and we didn't."

"Then the vandalism must have happened around sunset, between six o'clock and six-thirty," Hawkeye concluded. "And almost anybody had the opportunity. So next, we need to examine motive. Who *wanted* the statue broken?"

"I don't think anybody wanted it broken,"

said Deputy Mayor Drummond. "I think it was broken accidentally and that Mrs. West is the culprit. She probably broke it while she was cleaning yesterday." All eyes turned toward Mrs. West.

"Well! I never!" protested the cleaning woman. "In fact, Deputy Mayor Know-It-All, I wasn't even at work yesterday. I was home with my little girl, Trudy. She was getting over the flu, and I wouldn't have left her for a minute. If you're so eager to find someone for them to suspect, why don't you explain to these nice people why you made an ugly face every time you looked at that statue of Mr. Forthwit!"

Drummond looked stunned as the group turned to him. He composed himself and explained. "It's true that I didn't like the statue. I've always thought it was unfair that Forthwit's statue was in City Hall, but there's not even a painting of my great-grandfather, Josiah Drummond. He was Forthwit's partner and the real brains of their trading business.

"However, let's be reasonable. I was in a meeting with the mayor. Anyway, how could I benefit from the destruction of the statue? You should look for someone who has something to gain. How about that man?" He pointed to Martin Grafton, the artist, then continued. "For years, Mr. Grafton's painting has been hidden behind the Forthwit statue. Now it's visible to everyone!"

"Just a minute!" said the artist angrily.

"You've got no right to accuse me of anything."

"Calm down, everybody," said Sergeant Treadwell. "Mr. Grafton, is there any way you can prove that you weren't here yesterday evening at six o'clock?"

The artist suddenly looked smug. "As a matter of fact, Sergeant, I *can* prove it." He pulled a photo out of his pocket and passed it around the group.

"At sunset last night, I was all the way over in Earlham, forty miles from here, testing the delayed-action shutter on my new camera. There's the Earlham Town Hall in the background. I couldn't have been there *and* here at the same time!"

"How do we know this picture was taken last night?" demanded Sarge.

Hawkeye squinted at the photograph. "Look, Sarge. He's got a newspaper in his hand. I can't read the date, but the headline is definitely the one in yesterday's paper." Amy peered over his shoulder at the photo.

"And I thought this was going to be an *easy* case," said Sarge. He turned to Amy and Hawkeye. "Well, my young geniuses, what do you think of this? Maybe I should call in the lab boys and have them check for fingerprints, or else—"

"Whoa, Sarge," said Amy, looking up from Grafton's photograph.

Sarge blinked. "Don't tell me you've got this

"How do we know this picture was taken last night?" demanded Sarge.

one figured out! I don't believe it!"

"Sure," said Hawkeye. "You just have to keep in mind that alibis aren't always what they look like!"

WHAT MADE HAWKEYE AND AMY SUSPICIOUS?

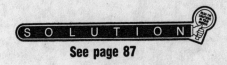

See page 87

The Mystery of Hawkeye's Letters

Dear Amy,

Here I am at MicroCamp, and already there's a mystery to solve: how could a smart kid like Hawkeye Collins (yours truly) pack so carefully and still forget to bring any shirts? My counselor, Jackson, made every other boy in my cabin lend me one. Today I'm wearing a shirt that says "San Gennaro Festival" on one side and "I'm Proud To Be Italian!" on the other.

Camp is neat. We spend three hours a day with computers. The rest of the time is spent on the usual camp stuff—hiking and sports. Tonight we're going on a sleep-over in the woods.

We all have to send one electronic-mail letter a day. You and my family will both get some. Also, we each have a special project to work on. Mine is an electronic sketch pad—of course!

Now I'm going to pack my stuff for the sleep-over. Hope I can remember to take a shirt!

Yours electronically,

Hawkeye

Dear Hawkeye,

Obviously, you should have asked me to help you pack. I would never forget the shirts. However, it does remind me of the time we went to New York on vacation and I forgot to take any shoes!

Can't write more now. I've got a baby-sitting job.

Electronically yours,

Amy

Dear Amy,

Now we have a *real* mystery! While we were away on our sleep-over, our computer cabin was vandalized. What a mess! Here's the story.

We left yesterday morning and hiked for about five miles to the far end of the lake, where we set up camp. A truck brought the tents and food and s'mores. All we really carried were our own sleeping bags and things. It took about two hours to set up camp, and most of that time was spent putting the food in raccoon-proof places.

That turned out not to matter because it wasn't the raccoons who got our food. While we were sleeping, a bunch of kids from Camp Rappahonk—a tennis camp—paddled across the lake, snuck up on us, and ripped off our food. One of our campers woke up and saw them just as they were making their getaway.

A guy named Bones Harkness spotted them. He used to work at MicroCamp before the director found out he was stealing software, and fired him. Bones said he had come to visit my counselor because they were such terrific friends. Jackson was the one who discovered that Bones was stealing the software, but Bones kept saying that he wasn't angry with Jackson.

Anyway, it was a good thing someone saw the Rappahonk boys. Otherwise, we would have blamed the raccoons for stealing our food.

In the morning, we packed up and came back to MicroCamp—to find our computer cabin a disaster area!

I've got archery now. I'm doing an electronic

sketch of the computer cabin, and I'll send it tomorrow.

Yours electronically,

Hawkeye

Dear Hawkeye,

What are you doing about the kids from Rappahonk? What is/are s'mores? And can you train raccoons to do dishes?

Electronically yours,

Amy

Dear Amy,

I don't think you can train raccoons to do dishes, but I *do* think they're trying to join the computer age! Look at this computer sketch. I'm pretty sure it was the raccoons who vandalized the place. They made a terrible mess—really pointless stuff. The printer was jammed, and paper was thrown all over the cabin.

Some of the guys thought it was another prank by the Rappahonkers, but I don't agree. The

"I'm pretty sure it was the raccoons who vandalized the place," Hawkeye wrote. "They made a terrible mess."

cabin has an electronic-eye alarm. It's on the door, about 18 inches above the floor, and it wasn't triggered. The Rappahonkers couldn't possibly know about it, but the raccoons wouldn't need to. They'd walk right under it!

I guess the kind of person who goes to New York barefoot is the kind who doesn't know what s'mores are. But you're a detective—you figure it out!

Yours electronically,

Hawkeye

Dear Hawkeye,

I found out what s'mores are, and I also figured out who your computer room bandit is! You're blaming the raccoons unfairly. Get the picture?

Electronically yours,

Amy

WHAT CLUE DID AMY SPOT THAT HAWK-EYE MISSED?

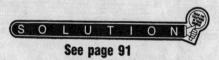

See page 91

SOLUTIONS

The Secret of the Fortune-Teller

"The only thing Madam Bertha saw in her crystal ball was what she'd already seen in Marie's note," Hawkeye explained to Mrs. von Buttermore. "When you looked at the note, all you noticed was her poor spelling. But there's a hidden message in this note.

"Look at the first letter of each word after your name. Those letters spell out DOG HIT BY CAR. And then there's the P.S., with the most important information for Bertha: RICH!"

"Oh, no!" said Mrs. von Buttermore. "What a fool I've been! I'd better call the police. I certainly don't want anybody else to get fooled by Madam Bertha."

"I'm afraid somebody else already has been fooled," said Hawkeye. He meant Mr. and Mrs. Selden.

When he heard Mrs. von Buttermore use the words hunky-dory in her Madam Bertha imitation, Hawkeye recognized it as the same odd phrase that Mr. Selden had used when talking to Amy's mother. Then when he learned that Mrs. Selden had been sitting next

continued

65

to Mrs. von Buttermore at Jean Pierre's, he was sure he knew why Mr. Selden had canceled his operation.

Right after Mrs. von Buttermore notified the police, Amy called her mother so Dr. Adams could talk to Mr. Selden and save him from a terrible mistake.

When things had calmed down a little, Mrs. von Buttermore tried to thank Hawkeye for his help, but she was interrupted by a phone call. It was the vet, Dr. Rodrigues, reporting that Priceless would make a complete recovery—without the aid of a crystal ball!

The Mystery of the Circus Kidnapping

"I knew there was something wrong with the makeup table," Hawkeye explained to the circus owner. "But I couldn't put my finger on it. Then I realized that was exactly what the problem was. Everything was backward. Look at the back slant of the handwriting and the position of the makeup, brushes, and scissors. The last person to put on his makeup must be left-handed. The last one to put on makeup would have been the last one out of the trailer, and no one would have seen him tape up the note."

Hawkeye and Amy had watched the clowns play baseball. When the clown named Lefty was at bat, he was true to his name. Only about seven people in a hundred are left-handed. So with eight clowns, the chances were that there was only one lefty. Hawkeye was right—Lefty was the only left-handed clown.

Hawkeye, Amy, and Ms. Wosniak spoke with Lefty during the intermission. The clown freely admitted that he'd taken the pony. "But it was only a joke," he explained. Then he led

continued

them to Peg, who was happily munching oats in the workhorse tent.

When the police arrived, Lefty got a lecture and a warning never to do anything like it again. He realized that his joke really wasn't funny at all.

Lefty apologized to Rosalita. She was still angry with him, but she did have the sense to apologize in return for putting soap in his shoes the week before. They agreed that the jokes had gone too far and that they'd try to be better friends from then on.

When the show was over, Hawkeye, Lucy, and Amy went to see Rosalita. After thanking them for finding Peg, she offered Lucy a pony ride.

While Amy watched her little sister bounce joyfully along on Peg, she decided that bringing Lucy to the circus had turned out to be interesting after all!

The Case of the Invisible Burglar

"Look at this, Hawkeye", said Amy.
"There's a large air vent at the back of the
China Closet store. No wonder all the people
on Summer Avenue didn't see the burglary.
It was taking place at the back of the store,
off the alley."

When Sergeant Treadwell went across
the street and examined the air vent, he found
that it was, indeed, how the burglar had en-
tered. The officer then came back and
challenged Amy to name the criminal.

"I can't name the burglar for sure, but
I have a pretty good suspect in mind. Think
about it, Sarge", Amy said.

"Hawkeye's sketch showing the air vent
is the same view that Mr. Fortunati sees all
the time when he's behind the counter here
in the restaurant. If he'd been here last night,
he would have spotted the burglar immediately.
But someone arranged for Mr. Fortunati to be
somewhere else last night. Someone made
sure that he would be busy all evening and
that Pronto Pizza would be closed."

"Ellen Markville!", yelled Hawkeye,

continued

73

Sarge, and Mr. Fortunati together.

Amy nodded. "Maybe it was only a coinci-dence that the radio commercial had to be recorded last night, but it was certainly a handy coincidence for the burglar."

While Hawkeye and Amy dug into their pizzas, Sergeant Treadwell hurried off to have a talk with Ellen Markville. He telephoned the restaurant a short while later to say that Amy had been absolutely right. Ms. Markville had confessed to the burglary and produced the figurines hidden in her apartment. She had wanted to add these figurines to her collection but couldn't afford them.

"Oh, dear. I thought all along that she really meant it about my perfect radio voice," said Mr. Fortunati.

Amy consoled him. "Mr. Fortunati, I don't know about your radio voice, but you do have one thing that's perfect—your pizza recipe!"

The Secret of the Video Game Scores

When Amy looked at Hawkeye's sketch, she saw her initials, AAA, in second place. She also saw that Toni Jane Adams (Toni—TJA) had moved up considerably, from seventh place to fourth place, and had broken 30,000 points. It wasn't having a sore throat that had kept Toni from raking leaves—it was being a sore loser! While Amy had been working, Toni had been at the arcade, practicing.

The next day, Amy got to the arcade at 1:00, as she and Toni had agreed. When Toni hadn't shown up by 1:30, Amy called her. She could barely hear her cousin's voice on the other end of the phone, but it was Toni.

Amy's aunt came on the phone and explained that Toni had a very high fever and terrible laryngitis and couldn't even leave the house. "It must have been from all that work raking leaves yesterday," she explained. "I hope you don't catch it, too, Amy."

"Oh, I don't think I will," said Amy.

By the end of the day, Amy had collected a blue ribbon in the derby, and the ratings had changed again. AAA was number one!

The Case of the Escaped Convict

"Here, look at my sketch of the kitchen," Hawkeye said. "If just Diane and her mother were going to have dinner together, why were there three sets of silverware on the table?"

"Right on, Hawkeye!" said Amy.

Sarge shook his head. "I thought that Mrs. Simpson was just a bit fast to suggest Mexico to me. I mean, it was like she already knew the answer before she got the question. But what do you think is going on?"

"I bet that either Mr. Simpson is there now, or he will be in time for dinner. And they must all be leaving soon—but not for Mexico." Hawkeye paused, then went on. "It seems odd that Diane is airing her winter clothes now, in June. Most people do that in the fall. The Simpsons must be planning on going to some place like South America or Australia, where it's the winter season now."

Sarge called the state police to surround the Simpson house, and Mr. Simpson was caught. Before he was sent back to prison, however, the police found three airplane tickets on him—to Australia!

79

The Mystery of the Speedy Snitcher

Amy suddenly noticed that the railroad tracks ran almost directly past Sun 'n' Fun and City Hall. All Bad News had to do was to wait for a train to approach, snatch the money, and hitch a ride on the train. Then he hopped off the train near City Hall and established his ironclad alibi.

Under questioning by Sarge, Bad News admitted that that was, indeed, the way he'd pulled off the robbery.

"I've been practicing jumping on and off trains for a couple of weeks now, outside town, where nobody would notice," he said proudly.

"You're lucky you didn't lose a leg—or have something worse happen to you," replied Sarge. Bad News had to go to court. Sarge Treadwell asked for a light sentence, and the judge agreed. Bad News went to the new State Rehabilitative Facility, where he got counseling and started studying diesel mechanics. He learned that any more bad news would mean a speedy trip to reform school or jail.

The Case of the Convenient Car Crash

"Look, Dad. In the picture, you can see the cast on Mr. May's broken leg.".

"So?"

"It's on his left leg.".

"Of course", said her father. "That's the leg he broke!"

Amy shook her head. "Then he didn't break it in your car accident.".

Captain Adams studied the photo. "Uh-oh, I think I see what you're driving at.".

"Well, it's really what you were driving at. Since Mr. May was on the passenger side, the only leg that could have been between the door and seat would have been his right one! I think we'd better find out what else happened to him that day!".

When Hawkeye's father called the injured man and confronted him with the evidence, Mr. May confessed that it had been a trick. He had broken his leg after the car accident, while playing with his children. He was desperate without money or a job, and he thought he could pretend he had been hurt in the car accident. He didn't mean to hurt

continued

Captain Adams. He just hoped to get some money from the insurance company.

While Captain Adams was very upset that he'd been tricked, he could understand someone lying because he wanted to feed his family.

A week later, Captain Adams got Mr. May a job at the airport as a ticket agent—a sit-down job until he could get back on his feet.

The Secret of the Smashed Statue

"It's not really hard to understand," said Amy. "Here we have three alibis, all of which seem airtight—at first. Deputy Mayor Drummond's story is pretty convincing. After all, he was with the mayor. But if we looked into it closely, we'd probably find that there was a break in their meeting when he could have smashed the statue.

"Next we have Mrs. West. If she'd wanted to, she could have left Trudy for a few minutes and come here to smash the statue. Nobody would have noticed, except maybe her daughter.

"Then there's the really airtight alibi. Not only was the artist, Mr. Grafton, miles away, but he has a photograph to prove it. How convenient that he was carrying it just when he needed it the most! A little too convenient, if you ask me. Right, Hawkeye?"

"Right. So Amy and I looked at the picture a little harder. In the photo, there's a sign at the crossroads: SMITH'S FARM. FRESH EGGS. TWO MILES SOUTH—with an arrow. Well, if south is to your right, as it is in this picture,

continued

87

then you're facing east. The sun doesn't set in the east, as it appears to be doing in this photo. It rises in the east. This picture wasn't taken last night at sunset, but this morning at sunrise!"

After some sharp questioning by Sergeant Treadwell, Mr. Grafton admitted his guilt.

"I just couldn't stand to see my painting hidden by that statue any longer. But I felt terrible as soon as I'd smashed it. I actually came here this morning to offer to repair it. I'm a sculptor, too."

"Hmmm," said the deputy mayor. "I think we have an opportunity to right two wrongs. If you repair the statue, that will certainly make up for your vandalism. And I think we could forget the whole thing if you'd do one more statue—of Josiah Drummond!"

Mr. Grafton eagerly agreed.

89

The Mystery of Hawkeye's Letters

Dear Amy,

What are you talking about?

Yours electronically,

Hawkeye

Dear Hawkeye,

When I looked at your sketch, I saw the same pointless mess you did. But look at the tear in the screen door. It's a neat U-shape. Raccoons couldn't do that. They'd have to bite and chew, and the tear would be rough and irregular. Of course, you're right about the Rappahonk boys. They'd never know about the alarm. Besides, this vandalism is vicious, not like campers' practical jokes.

It is what you might get from someone who has been fired. And someone named Bones can probably squeeze under an electronic eye—especially if he knows it's there!

When Bones Harkness showed up at
your campsite, he could have been trying to
establish an alibi for that night.
Think about it!

Electronically yours,

Amy

Dear Amy,

You are something else! I showed Jackson your letter, and he took it to the camp
director. They confronted Bones with the evidence, and he confessed! He wanted to get
back at Jackson and MicroCamp.
Everyone here is impressed with your
sleuthing. I told them you were just trying to
take a byte out of crime!

Yours electronically,

Hawkeye

Dear Friend:

Would you like to become a member of the Can You Solve the Mystery?™ Reading Panel? It's easy to do. After you've read this book, find a piece of paper. Then answer the questions you see below on your piece of paper (be sure to number the answers). Please don't write in the book. Mail your answer sheet to:

Meadowbrook Books
Dept. CYSI-L
18318 Minnetonka Blvd.
Deephaven, MN 55391

Thanks a lot for your replies—they really help us!

1. How old are you?
2. What is your first and last name?
3. What is your address?
4. What grade are you in this year?
5. Are you a boy or a girl?
6. Where did you get this book? (Read all answers first. Then choose the one that you like best and write the letter on your paper.)

6A. Gift	6E. Public library
6B. Bookstore	6F. Borrowed from a friend
6C. Other store	6G. Other (What?)
6D. School library	

7. If you chose the book yourself, why did you choose it? (Be sure you read all the answers listed first. Then choose the one that you like best and write the letter on your paper.)

7A. I like to read mysteries.
7B. The cover looked interesting.
7C. The title sounded good.
7D. I like to solve mysteries.
7E. A librarian suggested it.
7F. A teacher suggested it.
7G. A friend liked it.
7H. The picture clues looked interesting.
7I. Hawkeye and Amy looked interesting.
7J. Other (What?)

8. How did you like the book? (Write your letter choice on your paper.)

8A. Liked a lot   8B. Liked   8C. Not sure
    8D. Disliked   8E. Disliked a lot

9. How did you like the picture clues? (Write your letter choice on your paper.)

9A. Liked a lot   9B. Liked   9C. Not sure
    9D. Disliked   9E. Disliked a lot

10. What story did you like best? Why?

11. What story did you like least? Why?

12. Would you like to read more stories about Hawkeye and Amy?

13. Would you like to read more stories about Hawkeye alone?

14. Would you like to read more stories about Amy alone?

15. Which would you prefer? (Be sure to read all the answers first. Then choose the one you like best and write the letter on your paper.)

15A. One long story with lots of picture clues.
15B. One long story with only one picture clue at the end.
15C. One long story with no picture clues at all.
15D. A CAN YOU SOLVE THE MYSTERY?™ video game.
15E. A CAN YOU SOLVE THE MYSTERY?™ comic strip.
15F. A CAN YOU SOLVE THE MYSTERY?™ comic book.

16. Who was your favorite person in the book? Why?

17. How hard were the mysteries to solve? (Write your letter choice on your paper.)

17A. Too easy   17B. A little easy   17C. Just right
    17D. A little hard   17E. Too hard

18. How hard was the book to read and understand? (Write your letter choice on your paper.)

   18A. Too easy   18B. A little easy   18C. Just right
      18D. A little hard   18E. Too hard

19. Have you read any other CAN YOU SOLVE THE MYS-TERY™ books? How many? What were the titles of the books?

20. What other books do you like to read? (You can write in books that aren't mysteries, too.)

21. Would you buy another volume of this mystery series?

22. Do you have any suggestions or comments about the book? What are they?

23. What is the volume number on this book? (Look on the front cover.)

24. Do you have a computer at home?

ORDER FORM

Name _____

Address _____

City _____ State _____ Zip _____

Please charge my ☐ Visa ☐ Mastercharge Account

Acct.# _____ Exp. Date _____

Signature _____

Check or money order payable to Meadowbrook Inc.

Qty	Title	Cost Per Book	Amt
	#1 The Secret of the Long-Lost Cousin	$2.75	
	#2 The Case of the Chocolate Snatcher	$2.75	
	#3 The Case of the Video Game Smugglers	$2.75	
	#4 The Case of the Mysterious Dognappers	$2.75	
	#5 The Case of the Clever Computer Crooks	$2.75	
	#6 The Case of the Famous Chocolate Chip Cookies	$2.75	
	#7 The Mystery of the Star Ship Movie	$2.75	
	#8 The Secret of the Software Spy	$2.75	
	#9 The Case of the Toilet Paper Decorator	$2.75	
	#10 The Secret of the Loon Lake Monster	$2.75	
	#11 The Mystery of the Haunted House	$2.75	
	#12 The Secret of the Video Game Scores	$2.75	
	TOTAL		

We do not ship C.O.D. Postage and handling is included in all prices. Your group or organization may qualify for group quantity discounts: please write for further information to Direct Mail Dept., Meadowbrook Inc., 18318 Minnetonka Blvd., Deephaven, MN 55391.

18318 Minnetonka Boulevard • Deephaven, MN 55391 • (612)473-5400